Anne was born in Devon but the family moved shortly afterwards to a 60-acre farm in Essex. Anne had a happy childhood with her sister on the farm. Anne's sons and then grandchildren were a captive audience for her love of storytelling. Anne has many interests from horse riding, where she competed at many county shows, to archaeology. Also, her love of history where she has lectured to audiences at several venues relating to life in the Tudor period. Anne then inherited the farm and lives there with her husband and the animals.

Anne Mowling

MY NAME IS SAVANNAH

AUSTIN MACAULEY PUBLISHERS™

LONDON · CAMBRIDGE · NEW YORK · SHARJAH

A CIP catalogue record for this title is available from the British Library.

ISBN 9781398486041 (Paperback)
ISBN 9781398486058 (e-Pub e-book)

www.austinmacauley.com

First Published 2022
Austin Macauley Publishers Ltd®
1 Canada Square
Canary Wharf
London
E14 5AA

My thanks to David Button for all his help with the technical details

My thanks to Tracey Wheatley for her support

Lastly, my thanks to Christine Playle for her encouragement

My name is Savannah. I was born in a derelict barn on the Island of Phossoss, Greece, and I am a puppy. Mother goes away for a couple of hours for food each day, but always comes back to feed us. Now my eyes are open, I can explore this building which has no door and much of the roof has fallen in. There is a pile of old clothes in the corner, nice to curl up on. When it rains, at least we can lap up some of the puddles which form. There is a broken mirror in the corner, and for the first time I can see myself.

I certainly take after Mother with my short coat of golden brown, black nose, long tail and beautiful long blond eyelashes framing my golden eyes. No other markings apart from, what I seem to have, a very small black mark on my shoulder; a bit like a birthmark.

Whereas looking at my two brothers, who must take after their father, they are a mixture of black white and a splash of gold. No, I am most certainly the pretty one.

I see people walking past the building, but I always hide in the corner. Very occasionally, they drop some food on the path outside and Mother waits for them to walk by, before venturing out.

The days pass by, and I am now almost five weeks old. Mother has gone for food.

It's getting dark. *Where is Mother? We are all getting very, very hungry.* I expect she has been going out further to find food. Of course, she will be back, she wouldn't just leave us. We will just wait quietly. It's getting darker and still no Mother. We curl up on the pile of clothes waiting waiting waiting.

It's now daylight. Something is very, very wrong. My brothers start whimpering, and I tell them to be quiet. We patiently wait another day and night and still no Mother. What could have happened to her? Maybe she has fallen off the edge of the cliff and has hurt herself. Maybe she has been run over by the cars or bikes on the Island. All these thoughts race through my head. I won't start worrying too much, she will be back.

Another long night has passed.

My brothers say they are going out into the big world to find food, and they ask me to go with them. No, I'm too frightened; I will wait a little longer. A fond farewell was said and off; my brothers go…

I spent another day in my home and then hunger gets the better of me. If I just cross the path outside and make for the shelter of the trees, maybe someone will drop some food.

Am I brave enough to actually cross the path? It looks a long way to those trees and bushes. I can do this. I am going to be very brave. I really can't stay here any longer… So with a quick burst of speed, I cross the path. I didn't time that very well, and I fell off the step and arrived at the trees and bushes in a tangle of dirt and leaves.

No one is coming along the path. *How long shall I wait?* I seem to have been waiting.

For hours, nothing. I feel as though I will just lie down and not wake up.

I feel so low, I don't care what happens now. I curl up in a little ball as, once again, night falls. I wake to the sun streaming in through the trees. I can't move. I'm too weak.

Just a minute! What is that noise? It's a lady walking past with a bag. *Shall I keep quiet and hidden or shall I whimper?*

I couldn't help it, before I knew what was happening, I started to cry.

The lady with the bag came over to see what the noise was. The lady made some funny sounds and then lifted me up and tucked me under her arm. Now what Mother always told us? To be wary of people. I think I will probably just give up and sleep in this lady's arms.

The next thing I know, I am in a house which has a roof and doors. The lady puts me down and offers me a bowl of water. *Oh! I feel better already.* The lady then goes to a cupboard and brings out some fish, which she offers me. *Food at last!*

The lady tells me not to bolt it down but I can't help it. I am on the verge of starvation.

Mother was wrong; this lady is very kind and offers me some biscuits. I try to tell the lady I am looking for Mother, but she doesn't seem to understand.

Two young children have just come into the house and are greeted by the lady. I think they are her babies. They see me and start to make a fuss. They are stroking and cuddling me and playing with me. This life is okay; I can be happy here.

A man has just come into the house and been greeted by all. He saw me and started to shout at the lady, but the children said they wanted to keep me as I was friendly and cute.

My tummy is very full. I suppose I'll just go into a corner of the room to relieve myself. Ah that's better.

The man starts shouting at the Lady again and then kicks me quite hard; it hurt.

The lady picks me up and rubs my face in the mess and takes me through the house to a garden outside. *Oh! I get it, I must relieve myself out here.* Also, I will keep away from the man.

The house is quite nice. The kitchen is where most of the family eat and relax. It has a large table and several chairs. Through a door which leads to a small room is where the man spends most of his evenings listening to the radio and reading his paper. The children spend time in the garden, and when it starts to get dark, they go upstairs to the bedrooms. I am not allowed upstairs so I have no idea what it looks like. The nice lady tells me not to wander off. Just stay in the kitchen and garden. The lady says bad things will happen to me unless I stay here. I don't know what she means but it's best to do as she says. It's tempting to wander off just to see what these bad things are, but I am fed and looked after, even though I sometimes feel I would like to go for walks with the family. I often wonder why I can't go with them when they go out. Not that they go out very often. The children will go with their friends to a park or the beach. I look at them with my sorrowful eyes trying to ask them to take me along, but they just give me a hug and off they go.

Oh! How wrong can I be? The children have put a rope round my neck with a long lead and they are taking me for a walk. I hold my head up high as if to say to everyone, "Look at me, I have a family taking me out and about." The road, which is part sandy and part concrete, is very hot. Maybe this is not quite such a good idea because my feet are burning hot. I try skipping but that doesn't seem to make any difference. The children see my discomfort and take me onto the side of the road, which is grass. *That's much better.* We go a little further and the children stop at a shop and buy ice cream. *How lucky am I,* they have bought me one as well. Mmm, it's cold and refreshing, but I don't think I really like it that much.

The next day, the children take me out again. This time I have a smart new collar. It feels strange round my neck, but once again I hold my head up high as the passers-by stop to stroke me. The children seem very proud of me, especially with the compliments they are getting about me. This time they have taken me to a park. They put me on a swing and try to push it, but I quickly hop off. I don't like the swing. The children are laughing with their friends but I don't mind. I am getting a lot of attention. They haul me up some stairs and then they sit down at the top with me on their lap and we slide down to a mat at the bottom. *That was fun! Shall we do it again!* So the rest of the afternoon was spent going up the steps and down the slide. I like the park. I hope the children take me there often.

Time goes on, and I am now about five months old. The children are still very attentive towards me. Although school and their friends, I don't spend as much time with them now. Whereas the man seems to be spending most of his time at home and is always very angry. The man is pointing at me and telling the lady I will have to go. He is saying he has lost his job and certainly cannot feed me.

The lady starts shouting and arguing, as do the children. The man calms down and the lady sets the table for dinner, and I am thinking the matter is closed.

I will wander out to the garden and keep out of the way. It's a nice garden, long and narrow with high bushes either side. I can run up and down for exercise. There are some flowers on either side which have a beautiful scent coming from them. There is a shed to the side of the garden which the children keep their bikes and footballs in. The lady picks herbs from the end of the garden which she uses for cooking. I tried some of them. They tasted awful. The gate at the bottom of the garden is always kept closed, as there is a footpath at the end and the lady is worried I may come to harm if I wander off.

I can hear the family arguing indoors, so I get as far away as possible to the very end of the garden. I look and look again. The garden gate is open. Perhaps I could just have a wander outside until the family calm down.

I could just go a little way along the sandy path; I have never been outside without the family but with the unrest in the house at the moment, perhaps it's best.

This is going to be quite an adventure; I wonder where this path leads to.

Oh! There are several dogs all roaming along this sandy path. It's really nice to see other dogs, so I might just spend some time with them. Some are quite friendly and ask me to join in some sort of game they are playing. We chase butterflies. We never catch them, but it's fun leaping into the air. Other dogs snap at me and try to chase me away. I might just spend a few days with the nice ones and perhaps by the time I return to my home with the nice lady and her children, the tension in the household will be over.

I don't know how many days or weeks passed, but I felt it was time to return home.

I found my way to the house. It looked a little different. I couldn't think why it looked different. Just that it did. I barked at the back of the house as the gate was still open. Nothing, no one came out to see me. Perhaps they cannot hear me. I will go round to the front door and bark and scratch at the door. *Oh dear, I don't know how to get to the front of the house.* I must think this one out and find another way. When I used to go out with the children, they took me through the house and out of the front door onto the path.

When I followed the other dogs, days or weeks ago, there was certainly no turning to the front of the house. Ah! I remember I turned left. Now I will turn right. I am still on the sandy path which is quite familiar. I will keep going and see where it leads to. I now seem to be on a concrete path. I will try this new road. Not too good. There doesn't appear to be any way I can get to the front of the house. The houses all seem to be joined together; there must be a gap somewhere. Oh! Now I can see an opening down the side of one of the houses. Great, it leads to the front of all the houses. I make my way along the front and eventually reach the front of my house. I will bark and scratch at the door. Nothing. No one is in. Then I realised why the house looked so different. The windows were all boarded up; no one was living there.

So Begins My Life on the Streets of Phossoss

Phossoss is a small Island with water on all sides and a main street where most of the people seem to be. I think I will have a look round. *Oh! It's not too bad.* There are cafes, restaurants, and many shops. As I venture down the hill to the water, there are many many people, splashing about in the water. They have bright yellow rubber boats which the children are laying on. This looks like fun. I could just go and join in the fun with the children. *Why is everyone shouting and screaming?* They are throwing stones at me and talking about that dirty dog and its fleas. Oh well! Another lesson learnt. These people don't seem to like me very much especially in the water with them.

I will hastily go up the hill towards the main street.

Let me see what else there is on this island. I will keep off the main street and venture further on. I could, after all this time, see if Mother has returned to the derelict barn. I think I can find my way. I go past several buildings and a farm with goats grazing the grass. Well, nothing looks familiar to me. Maybe because of the nice lady who picked me up all that time ago, I have lost all sense of where I am. *That's an idea.* Thinking about the nice lady and her children, I have a good sense of smell; I could track them down. *Brilliant idea!* I bet they are looking for me. *Why didn't I think of this before?*

Before I go looking for my family, hunger has got to me; I need food. I will try the main street first of all. There are a lot of dogs and puppies waiting outside the restaurant. I will wait as well. Oh! There is a man throwing left over morsels of food outside. No chance. The bigger dogs have got there first and are making sure no one else gets a look in. I am quite shy, but I must eat. I push my way into the throng of dogs. *Bad idea.* I am now bleeding where they have bitten me. I will try something or somewhere else. I wander down to the beach looking for scraps that may have been left by the families that come down here. Not much in the way of pickings, but I see a Sandgrouse. I will creep up silently and try and grab it. As I get so very near, it sees me and flies up into the air. I leap with all my strength and yes! I have it. *What a tasty meal!* Even though the feathers are chocking me. I must remember this for food, although to actually get to the meat, the feathers really are quite unexpectedly tough to pluck out.

Now to find my family.

If I go back to the family house and try to pick up their scent, I should be able to find them. So I am outside the front door which is still boarded up. Now, using my acute sense of smell I wander slowly down the road. Ah yes! They have come along here. I wander for another ten minutes or so and then the scent abruptly stops. I will retrace my steps and start again. No good, they seem to have vanished from this point on the road. I look down on the ground looking for a hole they may have fallen into. *What am I thinking! Such a stupid thought.* I also look up into the sky. The hot sun must be getting the better of me, or I am just desperate! No matter, I am sure they are still looking for me, and we will all meet up.

I feel a little lonely, now I will find some nice dogs to play with.

I am quite a big dog. Well, I have long legs which make me appear bigger than I really am.

A little dog has come running up to me being chased by two rough-looking dogs. This is my chance to protect her. I have seen her around the Island but have always been too busy to speak to her. I rush in between her and the two rough-looking dogs. The two dogs look startled and, without more ado, they just wander off. I feel very brave that I have helped this little dog. The little dog rubs up against me and tells me her name is Bethany and that she was born on the streets of Phossoss and has always had to fend for herself.

This was my chance to have a friend and a purpose in life. I said to Bethany, "Let us stay together and we can help each other and in the cold nights cuddle up together." There were tears in Bethany's eyes as she said that would be the best ever. We must have looked an odd couple: me, a golden short coat, and Bethany a short-ish coat of grey, brown, white and black. A tiny girl who could stand under me, and often did in times of danger. I asked her if she would grow any bigger, but she said she doubted it, as she was three years old.

In the following weeks, we played, looked for food, and generally had a nice time.

There seemed to be a lot more dogs roaming the streets. *Where did they all come from?* After all, Phossoss was only a small Island. No matter, although food was getting really tight, and I knew I was getting thinner and thinner. We snapped and growled for our right to a morsel of food.

Bethany looked about her and said we must go as far away as possible. I didn't understand why this should be. Bethany explained that this time of the year, the holiday makers from other lands come here for their holidays. That sounded quite good to me. They would take pity on us and throw us some food. Bethany said, no, this was not the case. The people of Phossoss were always worried that the tourists might get bitten by one of the dogs, and that just before the season opened, a large van with several men rounded up many of the dogs and took them to a shelter. I asked Bethany what a shelter was. Apparently some kind ladies take the rounded up stray dogs and look after them until a home is found for them. That didn't sound too bad to me either. Bethany said it wasn't good, that although fed and watered, the dogs are kept in cages. I asked Bethany to explain. Bethany told me in detail that because there were so many stray dogs on the Island and when the tourists arrived, the tourists seeing so many dogs would, out of kindness, start to buy food for the dogs. Of course the dogs would get to know of this and would, more or less, become a pack, fighting amongst themselves for scraps. The tourists became very intimidated with so many dogs around them and started to complain to the authorities. I asked Bethany why there were so many dogs about.

Bethany said that for a few weeks in the year there was what people referred to as the hunting season. The men would take their dog along with many others, hunting for rabbits, woodcocks and wild boar this was allowed by the authorities for just a few weeks in the year... Worst of all, said Bethany, hunters came from other parts of Greece for the hunting season and when they returned to their own homes they just left the dogs to fend for themselves. I couldn't understand why the hunters would leave their dogs. Bethany said the hunters only wanted the dog for that particular season and then decided to leave them on the Island as it would cost too much money to transport them back to their homes and feed them for another year... Now I understood why there were so many stray dogs.

Once again Bethany took the lead and off we ran. As long as we were off the streets, Bethany assured, me we would be alright.

We found a sheltered old ruin to spend the night in. Once settled down, I asked Bethany that if the dogs went to the shelter and the kind ladies found a family home for them, why wasn't that good? The reply was that many dogs had not been found a home and were left in the shelter for months and sometimes years. Bethany said that the shelter was only able to continue with donations from people, mostly from other countries, as Phossoss was not a wealthy Island. So although we were always fighting for food, at least we were free to run and play.

I made a mental note to stay as much as possible away from the streets and just stay wherever Bethany said was safe.

The thought of being in a cage without Bethany brought tears to my eyes. I vowed to protect Bethany with all my power. Although really it was Bethany who looked after me.

We travelled all over the Island, mostly looking for food, which seemed particularly scarce. Making sure we kept well away from the main street.

I was telling Bethany about the park where the children had taken me. How I sat on their lap and how we slid down the slide to the bottom and then up the steps to slide down again and what fun it had been. We decided to go to the park;

it should be quiet by now as it was getting dusk. Bethany pointed out that the park was closed in the evenings so we would not be able to get in. I told Bethany to follow me as I knew a way. Once reaching the park which indeed was closed, I walked to the back of the park and there was the hole in the fence which I had noticed when with the children. It did not take us long to wriggle through the hole.

Now to the slide. I started up the steps which had quite large gaps from one step to the next and on looking round for Bethany I hadn't realised.

That Bethany could not get up the steps. Each time she tried she fell through the steps.

Bethany assured she would love to see me slide down. And she would wait at the bottom of the slide. Of course I wanted to show off. So up the steps I go and I am at the top ready to slide down. Bethany was watching I can't give up and look like a coward, but without the children helping me and letting me sit on their lap, it looked quite daunting.

Here we go. I sat as much as possible on the slide and before I knew it I was rushing down and landed with a bump at the bottom. Oh! The pain I felt as though my legs and body were on fire, but Bethany looked so impressed. I just stood up and with a shake pretended it had been fun. Bethany asked whether I would like to go down the slide again. I said that without her I felt selfish and we would leave the park before the warden came by.

There are a lot of sand dunes down by the beach and apart from the sandgrouse there were also rabbits. Bethany was quite good at finding any hidden rabbits and would burrow down one of the holes and scare the rabbits, and I would be waiting as they popped out. So although food was short and we were both always hungry, with Bethany's help, we didn't do too badly.

Oh! I see what Bethany means about the tourists. There are many strange people about but as long as we keep our distance, we should be alright. When it's tourist season, there are many small cafes and coffee shops open; so keeping our distance from people is the main priority. But on the up side, there are usually scraps of food to be had. The problem was that once the tourists left to go to their homes, the owners of the cafes and coffee shop would close up as there are not a lot of customers from the locals, so of course once again not much in the way of food about.

The sun is shining, and it's the hottest on record for this time of the year. So exhausting trying to either catch anything or find food. As Bethany points, out we are both getting thinner and thinner. I try my best for her but am finding it really hard.

I said to Bethany we really must venture onto the streets if we are to survive. At least there are the restaurants which usually throw waste food out the back of the building. Bethany agreed. So with reluctance but hunger pangs setting in, we made a dash for the main street.

There were of course several dogs also searching for food. With snarling, growling and all searching for any scraps of food, we joined in. Suddenly, Bethany started to sniff the air I wondered what on earth she was doing. "Follow me, NOW!" Bethany cried, which of course I did. We very hastily made our way off the street and down the hill towards the water.

Bethany explained that she knew the sound and smell of the van that collected the stray dogs to take to the shelter.

By now, we had made our way from the water's edge, up a hill where we could see from a safe distance the street we had just left. There we saw dogs and puppies being rounded up. The men and ladies collecting the dogs were kind and gentle, but we could see the fear in the eyes of those dogs. A lucky escape for us for the time being.

Next on the agenda was food. We could go back to the main street as the van had by now left. Bethany said to leave it for a while.

Standing on top of the hill gave us a good view for likely food.

I asked Bethany what all the pink birds were. "Surely they would make good food."

Bethany laughed and told me they were pink flamingos and to try to catch one would be impossible. She explained that when near to them, they were much bigger than looking at them from a distance. Also, they had sharp beaks and sharp claws and were always in or near the water.

We will try somewhere else for food.

By the sand dunes is where a lot of the sandgrouse seem to congregate. Although the feathers are tough to pull out, at least it's food. Nearby are tall grasses. As we walked over the grasses with eyes down searching, I stopped so abruptly that Bethany fell between my legs and with a laugh started to roll over. The reason I had stopped was just before me was a large nest of eggs. We were both overjoyed because a great meal lay before us. They were large eggs and much bigger than sandgrouse ones. No matter, it was a meal. We both wondered why the mother had forsaken them, as they were stone cold.

Night fell and as neither of us felt too well, so we decided to curl up by the side of the path. During the night, I woke to see Bethany being very sick. I also felt unwell. We both decided it must have been the eggs. No wonder the mother had left them. I started to get up to find water, maybe we would feel a little better. Bethany just lay there, so I decided to curl up with her and keep her warm and safe.

Two young girls were walking past and spotted us in the grass. They came over and looked at us and touched Bethany. They hurried on by and within a few minutes two older ladies came and looked at us. They lifted Bethany up, which made me growl. No one must take my Bethany away. The two older ladies spoke softly and reassuringly and between them lifted me up. *Now what??*

So Begins Our Life at the Shelter

At least we are together. The two older ladies carried us along the path and then out of nowhere another lady appeared with what looks like a wheelbarrow. They gently put us both into the wheelbarrow and proceed up the hill.

Neither of us are feeling any better but having reached a large fence, we both realise we are approaching the shelter. Bethany starts to shake, this has always been her dread. I try to reassure her. The two older ladies wrap us in blankets and put us in a cage. They then give us each a bowl of water. It doesn't taste like water, but we drink it down anyway. It is now very dark and all we want to do is sleep.

Morning has broken to the sound of many dogs barking. Bethany and I get up and stretch and walk to the front of the cage. Looking out through the bars, it doesn't look too bad but neither does it look too good. We are now feeling better. We can smell food and as three ladies bring us a bowl each, we down the much appreciated food before looking around to what and where we are. Our cage is narrow but goes quite far back which we found was of benefit in the hot summer days. The cages were constructed of concrete and bricks with iron palings along the front and a small door of iron. At the back of the cage was a pile of blankets, making a bed for both of us. Towards the front, a torn up carpet of newspaper.

The ladies of the shelter were all very kind and gentle and looked us both over for any signs of wounds and rubbed ointment into mine and Bethany's sores which we had gained through our journey on the Island.

I looked through the bars as much as possible to discover the cages were in a row of maybe twenty or so. In front was a surface of blocks of stone and then a tall fence.

Having finished our meal, we saw several dogs being let out of the cages and running loose along the path in front of us and the high fence. As we were new to the shelter, several of the dogs came over to investigate us. Now I could ask questions.

I asked how long they had been here, to learn that many had been in the shelter for months while a couple of them for years. I learnt that several dogs at a time were let out while the ladies cleaned their cages and put new shredded paper down. Also, that many of the holiday makers upon arrival at Phossoss would come straight to the shelter and take one or two dogs at a time on leads for a walk. That sounded wonderful, hopefully Bethany and I would soon be on a lead with the holiday people.

Oh! It's Bethany and my time to be let out of our cage, while the ladies clean it. Now I can see our surroundings instead of looking through the railings. Not much to see really. Although the high fence is also railings so I can look through at the beautiful Phossoss countryside which makes me sad but here at least we are not going hungry and different people throughout the day come and talk to us and give us cheese and ham as a treat.

I have become quite friendly with a large dog that appeared to be a bundle of nerves never staying still always pacing up and down when out of her cage, but a wealth of information.

Bethany and I were let out one morning with the nervous dog so we paced up and down with her to try to keep up and learn some more about what will happen to us. She told us that a photograph will be taken of each of the dogs at the shelter and these photos will then be put on a website which is sent to nearby countries. I couldn't understand why this should be but Missis Nervous who had all the answers informed me that this was how adoption worked.

She said people who were looking for a dog would look at the pictures on the website and make inquiries regarding a particular dog. So according to whether people were looking for small medium or large dog was whether you were the one for them. Missis Nervous had been here for several months but she had heard that someone was very interested in adopting her which made her pace up and down even more. I asked her why this has made her even more nervous, she said it was the unknown. Would the new family love her? Would they take her for walks? Would they let her run free? Would she be in the house or tied up to a kennel outside? I could understand how she felt, but there was nothing any of us could do.

Bethany and I have been here for a week now and cannot complain as we are fed and watered and made as comfortable as possible. We have been out on leads with the holiday makers only once but that was a lovely change. As the days pass, I have become more than a little frustrated as it's just so boring in the cage day and night. The ladies give us toys to play with but there is nothing to compare with running free over the hills and playing in the sand dunes. To take my frustration out I have decided to rip my blanket up to shreds. The lovely ladies never scold me and just keep renewing my blanket. Bethany scolds me as she has to share my blanket.

I cannot believe how very cold it is at night. Cool in the hot summer in the shelter but so cold at night. We are the lucky ones as we can cuddle up together for warmth.

There is one particular lady who has taken a shine to me and comes nearly every day to groom me and make a fuss of me with treats of the usual ham and cheese. Her name is Sindy and I wonder why she cannot adopt me, but by the conversations I hear, Sindy works at the nearby airport and would not be able to have a dog as she is away so often.

However her company is much appreciated even though I am always on a lead as at every opportunity I must admit, I try to escape. We have been on some nice walks together, with Bethany as well. I cannot believe there are parts of the Island that Bethany and I have never seen before, I thought we had explored everywhere but that's because we had always kept well away from the main roads and houses. Sindy knows everyone and on our walks we stop several times to speak to her friends. I just wait patiently. It's just nice to be out of the shelter.

It is particularly cold now at nights and the ladies have had some doggie coats delivered to the shelter from well-wishers from other countries. The smaller dogs love their coats as does Bethany but I prefer to rip mine to shreds. I do not like to be restricted in a coat.

The ladies have just come to the shelter with great news. There are eleven dogs for possible adoption.

Bethany and I are amongst them. We both got very excited then a little downcast as we don't know if we will be together.

I try to reassure Bethany that whether together or not anything is better than this life we are leading at the shelter.

I have just met up with Finn, a little dog who is so miserable that he makes me feel even more depressed. Finn is inside his cage as the ladies do not let the boy dogs and girl dogs out together. Probably because this causes fights. Finn tells me he will never be adopted because he only has one eye and who would want a scruffy dog with one eye?

Missis Nervous has passed us by with her usual pacing and actually stops to let Finn know that he is one of the eleven dogs destined for a new home. Finn practically does somersaults and of course is eager for more information. Missis Nervous can't stay still long enough and starts her pacing. Well that was the end of that conversation.

Of course I was eager to know how Finn lost his eye. Finn didn't really know what happened. All he could remember was, he was trying to catch a rabbit when there was a loud bang and that's when he found himself in the shelter. The ladies had looked after him but nothing could be done to save his eye. Even Missis Nervous who knows all the gossip, had no answer for how Finn lost his eye.

I felt so happy for Finn and hoped we would all be together when we travelled to wherever we were going, which was still a mystery to us all.

The ladies told us we would be going on a boat to take us to our new homes. I had never been on a boat and felt quite nervous about the whole ordeal, particularly when they also said we would be travelling in cages in a van. Eleven dogs in a van did not sound too good but to be in a family was worth all the hardship we would all be going through before reaching our destination.

Then we were told we had to have an injection to be able to go to another Country. I think I will try and tell Sindy that I don't want to go. *An injection? On a boat? In a cage? In a van? Many days travelling? Going somewhere strange?* Sindy assured me all would be fine.

The two drivers of the van who are taking us through our journey are, Len and Sam. They come to the shelter most days so we get to know them because the journey will take maybe as long as a week.

Len is the quiet one and is always gentle and softly spoken to all of us. Whereas Sam just wants to be with us dogs and loves to play with us. He has rather a loud voice but always makes sure we have the best attention from him. I have not had a good relationship with men through my life, but like all of us we always look forward to seeing Len and Sam with their usual tit-bits of ham and cheese.

The day has dawned and we now have collars with our names on them and are told this is the start of our journey. Several of the shelter ladies are here to help with placing us in the cages in the van. I look inside and wonder how we are all going to fit in. I see large cages and smaller cages. *So this is how we are all going to manage.* Missis Nervous and I are in the larger cages and Bethany and Finn are in the smaller cages. It is a tight squeeze but Bethany is next to me. I recognise several of the dogs. Best I get to know all of them as we shall be together for quite a long journey. No one is happy. We are all barking and whining but Lens soft voice reassures us. We are all loaded now and are told we are going to the port to catch the ferry.

Many of the shelter ladies are following us in their cars to transfer us from the van to the ferry. I do not understand why, but it will be nice to see Sindy again if only for a little while.

We have arrived at the ferry and the ladies take us on our leads out of the van and walk us up a very steep plank. So this is the ferry with its noisy and smelly engine. I do hope we are not on it too long. We are walked along the deck to the waiting van where many fond farewells are said. Sindy gives me an extra hug and tells me to be happy. Many of the shelter ladies have their favourites and there were many ladies leaving us with tears running down their faces.

So, Our Journey Begins

It was kind of the ladies to give us breakfast this morning but maybe a big mistake. With the heat of the engines and the smell of diesel and the rolling of the ferry, we are all sick. Not nice in a crowded van to say the least. I have quite a strong stomach, but it is all too much for me.

We were not long on the ferry and it is time to unload all the vehicles with us amongst them. Once off the ferry Len and Sam find a grassy patch along the road and one by one take us out and attempt to clean the van. Back in and it does smell a lot sweeter.

The ferry was taking us to the Main port of Greece. Oh no! We have now to catch a different ferry which will be taking us to Bari in Italy. We are on board, and this ferry is much bigger and nicer. Not much of a smell of fumes and doesn't roll as much as the smaller one.

By the time we land in Bari it is quite dark and we are all starving. Len and Sam feed us all and then once again find a quiet grassy place for us to relieve ourselves. Nearby is a fountain and Len has a large bottle which he fills with water and places a bowl for us to drink from. Then back in the van.

Len and Sam have not eaten and are both very tired. We travel for about 15 minutes and then the two men find a café.

One of them stays with us whilst the other goes in to eat and then they change over. All is quiet as we all fall asleep. Not comfortable for us but neither is it for Len and Sam. I think, but not entirely sure, that one of the men goes into the hostel for a good night sleep whilst the other one stays with us in the van.

Missis Nervous is such a bundle of nerves because she cannot pace up and down that she has taken to chewing the bars on her cage and is now complaining of toothache.

Morning at last and Len and Sam take us out to stretch our legs and feed us our most welcome breakfast. The men think we will be alright as we are now travelling by van.

Finn is the quietest of all and just puts up with everything. Never a whine nor a bark. As long as Bethany can see me she is fine but panics when I am taken out of the van without her.

Back in the van, and now we are off to Bologna in Italy. Everything is just a haze now as the journey has once again made many of us sick with the swaying of the van. Len and Sam say they are not going to feed us breakfast anymore but a large supper instead.

One day after another just merge into travelling for several miles then being taken out for a stretch and a drink of water and back in the van. I suppose we will eventually get to wherever we are going. Most of us are very very quiet and I tell Bethany to not give up as we surely are nearly there.

The van has a sliding door to one side and two doors at the back. Even so it is a mammoth task to get us out one by one to stretch our legs and then back into our cages.

Len has noticed that Missis Nervous's mouth is bleeding with her continual chewing the bars of her cage. Len puts some water in a bowl and bathes her mouth and then puts a muzzle on her. Better the muzzle than an infected mouth.

We are now travelling through France and the weather here seems a lot colder, but with eleven of us in a van it is still quite warm.

Sam has told us we are now going on a large ferry boat which will not be a long journey as Calais to Dover is not very far. It seems a long time, but in fact it was just over an hour.

We arrive at Dover and Len and Sam now tell us that several of us will be going north and some South. Those going north will be taken from the van and placed in another van and at last taken to their forever homes. Bethany and Finn are amongst those.

All that I have gone through all these years is nothing compared to seeing my Bethany taken from her cage and lead to a waiting van. I call out to her that she will be happy because she was actually chosen by a family.

I just hope that as both Bethany and Finn are small dogs that maybe they will both be adopted together by one family.

Now another long journey by road in the van. Len and Sam as usual stop several times for us to stretch our legs, they have both been so attentive the whole journey. A little easier now as there are only five of us.

I have time to reminisce and think of the good and bad times with Bethany. Mostly good times. Playing in the sand dunes, trying to find food, catching rabbits and the odd sandgrouse, the never to be forgotten episode in the park on the slide, cuddling up together in the bitter nights. Bethany rolling down the hill after I had so abruptly stopped. I miss her already.

Thinking also of my time with my family who I never ever saw again. The same with my brothers, meeting so many dogs at the shelter and the kindness shown by the ladies.

Missis Nervous is still in the van with me. I have time to really look at her as she is now in the cage next but one to me. I always thought I was quite a pretty dog but compared to Missis Nervous I must appear quite plain. Missis Nervous is the same size as me but a much slimmer build with a beautiful long silky coat of what I can only describe as a rich red in colour. Rather a plain head but the beauty of her coat makes up for that. Wherever her forever home is the family will have to have a lot of patience as she is still a bundle of nerves.

The van has stopped and not for us to stretch our legs. I am at my new forever home. I bid a fond farewell to Missis Nervous.

So Begins My New Life

Len slides back the side door of the van and I can see outside. I can see a large barn with hay in it and many ladies leading horses about. This looks a lot like a farm. I wonder whether this is good or bad, as many of the dogs at the shelter were from farms and were always tied up outside the house.

A man and a lady have come up to the van just as Len has opened my cage and put me on a lead. This must be my forever family, but I don't know them I want to stay with Len and Sam this is all too strange. I suppose I had better show them that I am happy to see them so I will jump up at the lady. Big mistake I have caught her off balance and she nearly falls over. Not a good start.

Len leads me down a path towards the house while Sam stays with the dogs in the van.

The man seems nice and makes a great fuss of me, the lady seems to hold back a little.

Len has taken my lead off and I can run around in the garden. I say run, I am so stiff with all the travelling in the van in the cage. I am finding it quite difficult, so slow down to a walk.

There is a lot of talking between Len and the man and then Len says he must make a move as he still has several dogs to take to their homes. I cry out to Len that I don't want to stay here with these strangers, and as Len closes the garden gate behind him I find a really small gap in the hedge and try to push my way through to get to Len. Now I am stuck and the man of the house helps me out of the bushes and finds some netting to stop that happening again. Len hesitates and then is gone.

The man puts me on a lead and says we are going for a walk across the fields. Then out of the house appears a black dog of about the same size as me. The black dog seems to be the boss of the house and much loved by the lady. The black dog is called Rain and I decide there and then that Rain will understand I am the boss now. After all I have had to stand up for myself and Bethany many times when in Greece, so it's best, right from the beginning, to let this dog Rain understand I will not stand for any nonsense. Rain understands and keeps her distance.

After one or two snarls at Rain, the lady decides that it was not a good idea to adopt me as her precious Rain is now cowering in the corner.

The man speaks sternly to me and I decide perhaps this might be a nice life here and I will, in time, make my peace with Rain.

I find walking across the fields really enjoyable, although I am very envious of Rain who is not on a lead and runs off wherever she wants to. We have now come face to face with about eight horses, some of whom are very curious while the others just continue grazing. I am used to horses although not loose like these. Where I came from, the horses are used for pulling carts for the farmers. The man takes me round many fields and then as the weather takes a turn for the worse he turns round and we head for home. I wonder whether the man realises I haven't had anything to eat for hours and hours!

Dinner time at last. This is a strange dinner, a mixture of meat and gravy and biscuits. *Oh well, it's food.* I gulp it down while Rain daintily eats hers.

The man then takes me out to the garden on a lead and also calls Rain. This is familiar, must not use the house as a toilet. The man has seen how I am with Rain and tells me that we are all going to bed now and as Rain and I are not getting on too well, I will have to go in a cage for the night. *No! No! No! I am not going in a cage ever again.*

I struggle to get away from the man trying to push and pull me into the cage. The man won; I am now in the cage. Once inside, I twist and turn and bite at the blanket and whine and growl and when Rain comes near to the cage to see what the fuss is all about, I try my best to push the cage over. I am very nearly successful and the man then decides to shut me in one room and Rain in another.

Morning at last. I wonder what this day will be like. Well I think it must be morning, but it is still dark. The man puts me on a lead. Precious Rain is allowed to be free. We go across the fields where all the horses are. I pull violently at my lead because there before me is a squirrel, a nice tasty dish. The man tells me no. I don't think the man realises that anything that moves is fair game. I didn't manage to catch it.

Breakfast time which is much the same as I had last night. I can't grumble as there is a large bowl full of food. I try to gobble it down as fast as possible and then I move over to Rain's bowl. Rain shies away from me and the lady starts grumbling and telling me it is not my food and tells the man it is not a good idea to have adopted me. The man explains to the lady that I probably had to fight for food on the Island and so I really don't know anything about sharing.

Not such a bad day as I can run in and out of the house into the large garden. Now the man has shut the door and I can't get out. Rain looks at me and then goes to the door and just goes through it. What kind of witchcraft is this that Rain can walk through a door!!

Rain then comes back through the door. Maybe that is why the lady loves Rain, Maybe Rain is a very special dog.

The man notices my bewilderment and goes to the outside of the door which leads into the garden and then starts calling me. I try to tell him I am not special like Rain, I cannot walk through doors. The man comes back inside and leads me up to the door and believe it or not, tries to push me through. I don't know what the man wants but I just lie down. The man leaves me alone. I decide to watch Rain very closely when she walks through the door the next time. I think I understand. There is a hole in the door with a sheet of something over the hole which is what Rain walks through. I could just try. I push at the sheet covering the hole and it moves, but I am frightened that I will get stuck, neither one side nor the other of the door. Rain has just walked through and no harm has come to her. I will try and follow. I push and push and I now have my head through the door. Shall I just keep pushing or is it best to back out of the door? I will back out of the door and then run at the sheet covering the hole and hope for the best. Not a good move as I have just banged my head on the door. I will try again with a gentle push. *Well, that's a surprise!* I am now the other side of the door. Problem is, I don't know how to get back inside. The man has just come in from the yard and praises me as he thinks I have found a way through the door. I try to tell him that I have tried and tried but unfortunately I am not magic like Rain. He goes inside and then calls me and puts his hand which, I can smell, contains sausages through the sheet. He has lifted the sheet and now I can get back inside. I think I will gradually get the hang of this magic. Rain has just walked through the door again. I can do this because I want to go outside in the fresh air, but I am too tired now so I will leave it until tomorrow.

The man puts both of us on a lead and takes us to a car. I don't mind going in a car as long as it's not to take me to another home because I am getting used to this life on the farm.

There before me is what looks very much like a sandgrouse and it's just sitting there in the hay barn. One massive pull on my lead and I have the sandgrouse in my mouth. The man is trying to pull it out of my mouth, but I have it very firmly. There are feathers flying everywhere. The lady is laughing and says I am not going in the car with all that blood and feathers. Rain jumps into the car on the back seat and the man is still trying to wrestle the sandgrouse out of my mouth and opens the boot for me to get in. I should have guessed, special Rain on the back seat and me in the boot. When I say the boot of the car, it is in fact behind the back seat and quite honestly there is plenty of room. I can look out of the window as well. In my panic at trying to jump into the boot the sandgrouse drops from my mouth. Everyone is happy.

We go for a ride in the car to a shop. The lady goes in and returns with several bags of food. The lady opens the boot where I am, to put the shopping in. Not a good idea as I start to rip open the bags. The shopping is transferred to the back seat. Rain of course doesn't touch it.

As long as I can see the man I feel fine but as soon as he goes into another room or out of sight I stress. I take my stress out on my comfort blanket which is now a mass of holes. The blanket is now in shreds so I start on my dog bed. I have not been allowed into the other rooms in the house because the lady is worried I might kill her beloved cats. I don't think I would as when I am in the garden I have seen them in their outdoor run, and they are kinda cute. We had cats at the shelter and I never took any notice of them.

Some people have just arrived at the house with three dogs. The dogs are let off their leads and are playing in the garden. They come up to me and try to play, but I don't know how to play. The lady with the three dogs throws a ball and tries to make me run and catch it. The three dogs run and catch the ball but I just wait by the man. The three dog lady is calling the man "Dad" so that must be his name. The dogs are little like Bethany but soo boisterous. I will just hide under the table next to Dad. Oh! Thank goodness the three dog lady has left in her car.

Dad has decided that when he and the lady retire to the front room after a hard day's work on the farm that he will take Rain and me into the other room. That is wonderful I can be with Dad in the other room. Dad has put me on a lead why? Rain of course just walks in. Quite a nice room and Dad has put some bedding on the floor for Rain and me. I understand now why I am on a lead, the cats have come into the room. I just don't take any notice of them but the lady insists I stay on the lead just in case I make a lung for her beloved cats.

Dad has decided it's time for bed, so leads me, and of course Rain follows into the large kitchen and then opens the door to the garden and tells Rain and me to go to the toilet. *Okay,* we both oblige. Then it's lights out for bedtime. I sleep quite well it's been an exhausting day.

We go for walks everyday over the fields and after a week, Dad has said I could run free like Rain, and he takes my lead off. *This is perfect*. I can now follow all those lovely smells that are in the hedges. Dad has walked on, and I have decided that the other side of the fence looks far more interesting. I can hear Dad call me but I cannot get back through the fence as I am now in a different part of the field. Dad is now whistling but I still carry on looking for a place to get through. Dad eventually manages to find a way for me to get back but I just run off again, hunting for whatever I can get. Dad is saying to the lady that he is going to find a dog trainer as he is worried I will stray and not come back to him when called. I don't think he realises that it's like being back in Greece when Bethany and I could roam over the Island without a care in the world.

The dog trainer has arrived and tries to make friends with me by giving me sausages as tit-bits. Then it's off we go, the dog trainer, Rain, Dad and me across the fields. Of course I run off following all those smells of birds, rabbits, squirrels, foxes and other dogs. The trainer calls me, but I take no notice. She sees me through the hedge and throws a large hard chain. Not that she is trying to hit me it's just a noise and it makes me take notice. Then she starts feeding me with the sausages. I really don't understand what this is all about.

The dog trainer then tells Dad to throw the chain on the ground to make a noise when I refuse to obey. Dad throws the chain and again that rattling noise and then the unlimited supply of sausages when I go back to Dad.

Maybe it's best to go to Dad when he calls me and be treated with sausages.

The dog trainer has indeed trained Dad very well and he only has to reach into his pocket for the chain and I know that if I go straight back to Dad I will be fed those sausages. We have no more need of the trainer.

I am still quite restless as I am not sure this is my forever home. I still keep tearing up my comfort blanket but I am settling down as much as possible. I have made friends with Rain and the tables have turned as Rain is now very much the boss. Well she knows her way around the farm so I just follow and all is well between us.

I am still contained in the garden which isn't as bad as it's a very large garden. I can of course seek out in the hedges anything which moves. The garden is surrounded by quite tall hedges and I can hear rustling inside. If I go inside the hedge I can see whatever is making that noise. I cannot get through the hedge as there is a wire fence all around the garden, however having gone into the hedge I am now stuck, so the only way out is up. Up I go and am now on top of the hedge. Dad comes out to see what all the noise is about. He can't stop laughing and is now taking pictures of me on top of the hedge.

Dad has decided that I can now go out of the garden gate and as long as he is in the yard I can also run free. This is marvellous as I can smell rats and mice. We had a rat problem at the shelter and quite honestly the cats were useless. Dad has just moved a pile of logs and out pops a rat, Before Dad knows what is happening I have it in my mouth, Dad seems very pleased and throws down the sausages which he seems to carry with him at all times. I prefer sausages to rats so have left the rat for Dad to take care of and I will have the sausages.

I will just explore round the yard and follow my nose. I can hear Dad calling me and I will go back to him in a while but not quite yet. I didn't realise there were so many fields, I will just explore one of them. They are not the fields Dad usually takes Rain and me on. The grass is very long and I can just about see over the top. What on earth is that I am up against? *Time to go back to Dad.* I leap up to get a better view, only to see a herd of horses coming at a very quick pace up to me. Can I run faster than those horses! Well… I have to. Back to Dad at last, that field is now out of bounds for me at least, for the time being.

Dad has decided to tidy up round by the dung heap. I will be there helping him because I know there will be plenty of mice and rats as nothing has been disturbed there for quite some time. Oh yes! A lot of rats scampering out. I will help by catching them. Oh no! What has happened, Dad is flapping his hands about himself and pulling at his hair, and is now with head bowed down trying to remove his jacket and is now running full pelt back towards the house. Now I can see why. There are loads of wasps, he must have disturbed a nest.

I will stay here to catch the rats. Bad idea, I am now running as fast as I can to catch up with Dad as I am now being stung. I have never been stung by a wasp before but I know why Dad is crying out as the stings really hurt. Dad is opening the freezer door and getting out some ice packs, he places some on his neck and arms and some on my stomach. They itch so much but the ice pack does make the pain go away, well, just a little bit. The stinging gets better but not until late evening and now it's time for bed. A restless night for Dad and for me.

Morning at last and the lady has just opened a gate into the front garden, I have not been in here before so I will explore. As I go in through the gate there is a squawking noise and a flurry of white rushing towards me. I had forgotten about the Ladies pet geese. A sharp bite on my back leg lets me know they don't like dogs. A hasty retreat is called for. The lady has some strange pets, the geese which are as big as swans, a snake, and some insects which look more like twigs from the trees.

The three dog lady visits us quite often and I have become quite friendly with her dogs. The three dog lady has given up throwing the ball and asking me to fetch it. What a waste of hunting time, why would I want to fetch a ball when there are so many trails to follow and so many scents!

We sometimes go in the car to a nature reserve where dogs are allowed as long as they are on a lead. I like it here as I have Dad all to myself as the lady takes Rain on her lead. There are a lot of swans here but they are in the water and there are people throwing bread out to them. Having gone all round the wooded area we then branch off to a path which leads to a small gate. Inside the gate are tables and Dad gets coffee for him and the lady and offers Rain and me the usual sausages. We just lie quietly under the table until Dad and the lady finish their coffee and then off we go back to the car.

Life goes on with all the ups and downs and I have been here on the farm for a year now. I am so lucky to have been chosen by Dad and the lady from the shelter in Greece. I could not be more grateful. I am sure there will be many more adventures but that will be another story…

Note from the Author

Bethany's new home was with a farmer and his wife and their five children. There were other dogs on the farm, but they were only allowed in the kitchen whereas Bethany was thoroughly spoilt by the children and was allowed wherever she wanted to roam. Even in and on the beds with one or other of the children.

Missis Nervous went to an elderly couple who lived by the sea. Whether it was the sea air or the unrequited love the couple had for Missis Nervous will never be known but Missis Nervous calmed down, stopped her pacing and enjoyed her life to the full.

Finn did not, in the beginning, fare so well and was miserably bullied by the couple's other dog. After a month, the young couple realised that the two dogs would never settle together. An elderly man who lived on his own had always stopped to pet Finn whenever he saw him. The young couple decided Finn would be so much happier with the man, and after a short discussion, the man with tears in his eyes took Finn to his house. Both elderly and scruffy of course; they were meant for each other. Finn was settled and very happy.